D0338653

RICHARD SCARRY'S
Great Big Schoolhouse
Readers

The Mixed-Up
Mail Mystery

Illustrated by Huck Scarry
Written by Erica Farber

STERLING

New York / London
www.sterlingpublishing.com/kids

Huckle and Bridget went
to the library.

Huckle loved trains.

Bridget loved mysteries.

When they went outside,
Skip didn't see Huckle.

Huckle didn't see Skip.

"Stop!" called Arthur.

Too late!

CRASH! The bike fell.

The boys fell.

Huckle's book went up in the air.

Something fell out.

It was a letter!

The letter was addressed to:

Miss Mouse
Cheese Street
Busytown

"Why is this old letter in my
train book?" asked Huckle.
"It's a mystery!" said Bridget.

They all went to Cheese Street.

They looked on one side
of the street.

They looked on the other side.

They did not find
Miss Mouse.

They did find Ella and Molly.
"We are looking for Miss Mouse,"
said Huckle.

Arthur bumped into Molly's bike.

The bike rolled away.

"Oops!" said Arthur.

Officer Flossy held up her
stop sign.

"Watch out, Lowly!" said Huckle.

Officer Flossy knew Miss Mouse.

She told them where to find her.

Miss Mouse was in her garden.

Huckle gave her the letter.

Miss Mouse read it:

Dear Miss Mouse,

Do you want
to get some
ice cream?

From,
Toot

"Toot Mouse works in the
train yard," said Arthur.

That gave them a great idea.

They all went to the train yard.

There was Toot!

Miss Mouse smiled at Toot.

Toot smiled at Miss Mouse.

"It has been a long time.
Do you still want to get some
ice cream?" asked Toot.

They all went to get ice cream.

"I love ice cream," said Arthur.

"I love trains," said Huckle.

"I love mysteries," said Bridget.

"I love you," said Miss Mouse.

And that was the happy end
of the mixed-up mail mystery.

STERLING and the distinctive Sterling logo are registered trademarks of
Sterling Publishing Co., Inc.

Library of Congress Cataloging-in-Publication Data Available

Lot #: 10 9 8 7 6 5 4 3 2 1
03/11
Published by Sterling Publishing Co., Inc.
387 Park Avenue South, New York, NY 10016

In association with JB Publishing, Inc.
121 West 27th Street, Suite 902, New York, NY 10001

Distributed in Canada by Sterling Publishing
c/o Canadian Manda Group, 165 Dufferin Street
Toronto, Ontario, Canada M6K 3H6
Distributed in the United Kingdom by GMC Distribution Services
Castle Place, 166 High Street, Lewes, East Sussex, England BN7 1XU
Distributed in Australia by Capricorn Link (Australia) Pty. Ltd.
P.O. Box 704, Windsor, NSW 2756, Australia

produced by ⬤JR Sansevere

4650 1697 8/11

Printed in China

Sterling ISBN: 978-1-4027-8450-7 (hardcover)
          978-1-4027-7321-1 (paperback)

For information about custom editions, special sales, premium and
corporate purchases, please contact Sterling Special Sales
Department at 800-805-5489 or specialsales@sterlingpublishing.com.